LAZY CAT

For Mr Toffee and Miss Kit-Kat, two very lazy cats

A TEMPLAR BOOK

First published in the UK in 2017 by Templar Publishing,
part of the Bonnier Publishing Group,
The Plaza, 535 King's Road, London, SW10 0SZ
www.templarco.co.uk
www.bonnierpublishing.com

ISBN 978-1-78370-643-3

Designed by Genevieve Webster
Edited by Alison Ritchie

Printed in China

LAZY CAT

Julia Woolf

t
templar publishing

Doodle Dog and Lazy Cat
lived together.

Doodle Dog tried his very
best to be a good friend
to Lazy Cat.

He played with Lazy Cat . . .

He shared with Lazy Cat . . .

But Lazy Cat didn't always try his best
to be a good friend to Doodle Dog.

And sometimes he was **very** lazy indeed.

One day Lazy Cat was as lazy as a lazybones
could possibly be.

Doodle Dog woke with a fright . . .

. . . and rushed to Lazy Cat's rescue.

"Mousey dropped out of the cat tree," mewed Lazy Cat.
"Fetch him for me would you, Doodle?"

Then . . .

"Can't reach my food," whimpered Lazy Cat.

"Carry me would you, Doodle?"

Just when Doodle Dog thought things couldn't
get any worse . . . they did.

"Telly's gone all fuzzy!
Fiddle with the aerial would you, Doodle?"

"Left a bit . . .

Right a bit . . .

Higher . . . higher!"

And Doodle Dog did. Until . . .

. . . he landed smack bang on the floor.
"Oooh Doodle, telly's gone all fuzzy again."

Doodle Dog had well and truly had enough . . .

And Lazy Cat had the feeling he'd gone
a bit too far this time.

So he decided to try and make it up to Doodle Dog.

"Look, Doodle, I've made you a delicious meal."

"Let's play scratching-the-sofa, then! It's so much fun!"

"Ok, how about sitting in a box . . . It's the best!"

"Ball of wool?"

"I know. Let's play hide-and-seek!"

Lazy Cat started to count.

Lazy Cat looked for
Doodle Dog . . .

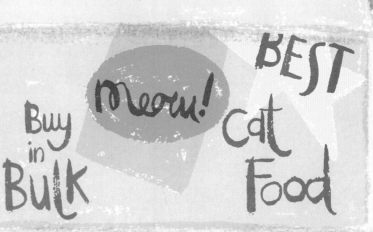

Buy in Bulk

Meow!

BEST
Cat Food

. . . but not very hard.

After a minute or two,

he stopped for a rest.

Doodle Dog waited
to be found.

He waited
and waited . . .

And waited.

Lazy Cat was **fast asleep!**
He **really** did have lazy bones.

But it gave Doodle Dog an idea . . .

And right now, a lazy cat suited
Doodle Dog just fine.